SPOOKY SAGAS

THE SOUTH WEST

Edited By Megan Roberts

First published in Great Britain in 2019 by:

Young Writers
Remus House
Coltsfoot Drive
Peterborough
PE2 9BF
Telephone: 01733 890066
Website: www.youngwriters.co.uk

Book Design by Ben Reeves

SB ISBN 978-1-78988-370-1
Printed and bound in the UK by BookPrintingUK
Website: www.bookprintinguk.com
YB0400Q

FOREWORD

Welcome, Reader!

Here at Young Writers our aim is to encourage creativity in children and to inspire a love of the written word. Each competition we create is tailored to the relevant age group, hopefully giving each child the inspiration and incentive to create their own piece of work, whether it's a poem or a short story. We truly believe that seeing their work in print gives pupils a sense of achievement and pride.

For Young Writers' latest nationwide competition, Spooky Sagas, we gave primary school pupils the task of tackling one of the oldest story-telling traditions: the ghost story. However, we added a twist – they had to write it as a mini saga, a story in just 100 words!

These pupils rose to the challenge magnificently and this resulting collection of spooky sagas will certainly give you the creeps! You may meet friendly ghosts or creepy clowns, or be taken on Halloween adventures to haunted mansions and ghostly graveyards!

So if you think you're ready... read on.

CONTENTS

THE SPOOKY SAGAS

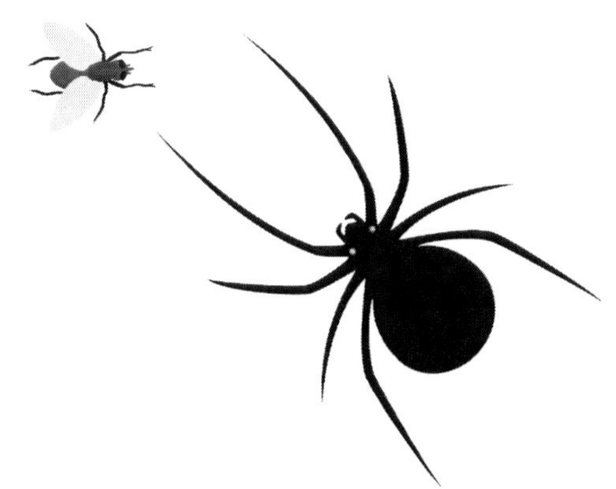

THE DAY I LEFT HOME

Once upon a time, there lived two little girls called Ayesha and Ella. Ayesha was going round to Ella's house. "Oh! I left my teddy!"
"It's okay," said Ella. "When you come round, I'll keep you safe."
When Ayesha knocked on her door, she heard some whispering behind her back. "I'm scared," said Ayesha worriedly.
Suddenly, a vampire came out of nowhere and took her away! Then she had no idea where she was. Then he tied her up and she was very scared. A ghost then rescued Ayesha and took her back home.

Grace Linfield (11)
Binstead Primary School, Binstead

HALLOWEEN HOWLS - A PAINFUL CHILL

The night before Halloween, four friends went camping in a forest. Eli suggested telling ghost stories around the campfire. The others thought it was a great idea, they did just that. Erin heard a noise and stood up to see what it was. Out of nowhere, a cute puppy appeared. It was seconds from midnight and the dog was alone. The clock struck midnight.
Suddenly, the dog howled and grew larger and larger. It was a werewolf! *Slash!* Erin's face spurted blood and a figure appeared. The werewolf jumped into his arms and they vanished with an evil laugh...

Aaliyah Smith (11)
Binstead Primary School, Binstead

THE HAUNTED HOUSE!

I thought I was just trick or treating, until I woke up and found myself in a haunted house.
"Where's my sister?"
I thought I'd lost track of her. I then soon realised this house was haunted.
A few minutes later, I wondered if the ghost took my sister as well as me and just put her in a different place. I later saw my shadow then, behind me, was a huge, dark figure lurking over me!
Later on that day, I found my sister. We found a potion on the floor and poured it over ourselves to get away.

Hayley Louise Molloy (10)
Binstead Primary School, Binstead

DR MURDER

As I awoke from my hospital bed, I realised there was no doctor at all. I could hear footsteps in the distance, but they were very quiet.
What felt like hours later, a man came and sat at the end of the bed with his back to me.
Trembling, I said, "Can I help you?"
Then suddenly, he turned around. His face was full of blood and not to mention he was holding eyeballs in each hand! I started shrieking, but no noise came out. Suddenly, I realised it was all a dream!

Elliot Apter (11)
Binstead Primary School, Binstead

DOLLS IN THE DARK

It was Matthew's birthday. Celebrating was him, Alex and Tom. "I'm not sleeping next to the basement!" shouted Alex.

"Neither am I!" screeched Matthew.

Tom said calmly, "I'll go."

As they got into bed, Tom heard a voice coming from the basement. As he slept, the door opened slowly. *Creak!* Something, someone, crept up to Tom. It had blood-red eyes, ruffled, ripped hair and held a knife dripping with blood. It was a doll! As it leapt on him, Tom let out a blood-curdling scream. The knife drove into his heart. Blood wept out of him onto the floor...

Lucas Payne (9)
Blue Coat CE Primary School, Wotton-Under-Edge

A SCARE IN THE NIGHT

Tom opened the door and stepped through. Suddenly, a screaming skeleton jumped on top of him! Tom pushed it away and stumbled backwards into a massive cobweb. He looked up to see ten red eyes staring down at him. He tore himself free and rushed downstairs into the lounge. He saw a huge, green, furry monster staring down at him.
He rushed back upstairs just as the landing light flickered on. "Stalky!" Tom yelled.
The freckled, short-haired boy in front of him laughed. "Gotcha!" he chuckled mischievously.
"I'm going to get you back for that!" Tom shouted loudly.

Harry Michael Fell (11)
Blue Coat CE Primary School, Wotton-Under-Edge

HAUNTED DOOM: VOLUME ONE

George slowly opened the door. It made a creaking sound as he entered. The crooked hall gave a spine-chilling feeling. "Oh my..." he murmured.

As soon as he stepped inside, the door slammed shut, trapping an echo as well as him. The labyrinth of halls mocked him as he wondered, "Someone? Anyone, please?" As sadness became fear and fear became panic, he starting sinking. "Just my luck," he groaned, forgetting he was also stuck.

Soon, the floor was at his knees. "Help!" he screeched. He was helpless. Soon the floor was at his shoulders. "Help me..."

Aodhan Peter Nickols (9)
Blue Coat CE Primary School, Wotton-Under-Edge

THE SLIMY SLEEPOVER

It was a dark, stormy night when Daniel awoke to a terrible noise. He wasn't sure what to do because he was staying at his friend's house for a sleepover. Daniel was too scared to see what the horrible sound was, so he snuggled back into his cosy, warm bed. "Whoo!"
There it was again! *That's enough!* Daniel thought. He peeped curiously under his bed and saw a green, slimy heap of sludge. "What is that?" he questioned. "A monster!" said Daniel. The trembling, ugly monster slowly slithered out from its hiding spot and Daniel jumped away in disbelief...

Edward Blaken (9)
Blue Coat CE Primary School, Wotton-Under-Edge

THE DEATH CRYSTAL

I'd finally found a wonder - the death crystal. I would make sure ghosts, vampires and skeletons would rise above humans. "Rise my friends, vampires, ghosts, skeletons! Ghosts and skeletons, destroy the buildings and, vampires, get the people and bring them back to me."

When the vampires came back, they came back with nothing. The humans followed the vampires and got out their weapons. I ordered the ghosts and skeletons to kill the humans, but they banished us all to the realm of death. People never saw us again, except for one little boy who, soon after, was never seen again...

Lewis Bennett (11)

Blue Coat CE Primary School, Wotton-Under-Edge

THE HALLOWEEN WOLF

It was Halloween morning. Freddie glanced out his window at the sparkling frost. "Ugh," sighed Freddie. "It's Halloween."
As it turned into the evening, Freddie sat waiting for trick-or-treaters. He sat patiently, watching TV. There was a knock at the door. Freddie opened the door and screamed, "Argh!"
A wolf was standing at his door! "It's only a costume!" said the wolf as he got up. Freddie's face was filled with fear as he gave the wolf sweets, even though he knew it was only a costume. Freddie ran to his mum!

Maddy Hall-Smith (10)
Blue Coat CE Primary School, Wotton-Under-Edge

THE LITTLE HOUSE OF HORRORS

It was a dark and ghoulish evening on the day of Halloween. Bats danced in the moonlight and owls hooted their chilling call. Anne was out trick or treating. She saw a spooky-looking house. Cautiously, she walked up to the door and knocked. The door swung open by itself.
"Hello?" Anne called.
She called out again. Nothing, only silence.
Then she saw a gleaming light moving towards her. It turned into a vampire and monster! She screamed, then turned and ran.
After a while, she turned and looked. The house had disappeared! She ran on until she found her friends.

Roo Young (9)
Blue Coat CE Primary School, Wotton-Under-Edge

HAUNTED HOUSE

A storm suddenly appeared out of the midnight sky. Tom was home alone in his old house.
Bring! Tom's telephone rang. *Bring!* Tom picked up the vibrating phone. "Hello?" he said.
No answer, so he hung up. Tom started to freak out, shaking. He reached his hands under his pillow to find a slimy, gooey piece of paper.
Bloody writing said 'Turn around' so, as scared as he was, he turned. Tom was relieved no one was there. He checked one more time.
Beaming red eyes overlapped the darkness!
After that night, Tom was never ever seen again...

Candy Chalk (11)
Blue Coat CE Primary School, Wotton-Under-Edge

THE LIVING NIGHTMARE

It started off in a little girl's bedroom. A whispering voice spoke, saying, "Get out!" She wondered what it was. It started to get louder, so she left the house. Then the girl went on an adventure. She had never been to the abandoned house near the graveyard before. She cautiously opened the door and looked around. Suddenly, all she could see were ghosts! The ghosts glistened in the darkness. All the girl tried to think about was that it was a horrifying dream. It wasn't working, but she realised the ghosts were coming closer.
"Argh..."

Lillia Grace Capener (8)
Blue Coat CE Primary School, Wotton-Under-Edge

AN EVENTFUL NIGHT

I awoke to an ear-splitting scream. I shot out of bed and turned to the door. Surreptitiously, I crept through the dark, silent hallway. Dark fog trailed from the unlocked attic entrance. Curiosity got the better of me. I found myself wading through the fog in the attic. Movement near the far wall caught my attention; I decided to approach it with caution. Screeches and moans filled the air. Piece by piece, a skeletal figure wearing a long, dark cape came out from the fog and slashed me. Suddenly, a wooden beam cracked the skeleton's head. The house gave way...

Toby Palmer (11)

Blue Coat CE Primary School, Wotton-Under-Edge

DEATH BITE!

One night, Jonny went to the supermarket. Later, when he got home, his mom wasn't in. Suddenly, he heard a freaky noise coming from the distance. He heard, "Jonny, Jonny! I want your liver!"
There was a dark figure on the stairs. He ran as fast as a cheetah. It was a half-headed granny, with a nightie full of blood! Jonny whispered, "Maybe she killed my mom!"
Jonny went to the front door. It was locked! He didn't have the key, so he jumped out of the window, stumbling as he hit the ground. He ran across the road...

Nina Blackburn (9)
Blue Coat CE Primary School, Wotton-Under-Edge

IT WAS JUST A DREAM!

In his gloomy, moonlit room, Monty was asleep. It was 3am and outside looked like outer space. Monty woke up and he quickly looked outside. There was the most terrifying thing he had ever seen - two round, bloody eyes staring at him as though he was some sort of food! Monty tried to let out a scream, but it didn't come. The eyeballs were knocking on the window. They were going to break through! More eyeballs appeared, looking even more terrifying than ever.
Monty woke up, it was just a dream! The eyeballs were really just the twinkling stars.

Max Petersen (8)
Blue Coat CE Primary School, Wotton-Under-Edge

ALL JUST A TRICK

Orlando, a nervous boy, slowly opened the screeching door. He peered inside. He set his eyes on a doll that was covered in ash, had lost its stuffing and had patches everywhere. Its face had a grinning smile. He looked away, but the doll was there and there and there... Suddenly, he heard footsteps, four pairs slowly getting closer. He hid in a corner. Then, all of a sudden, the lights came on. He could see his friends. Orlando told them about the doll, but they said they didn't do it. They ran out screaming, but the doll was there...

Fearne Anderton (10)
Blue Coat CE Primary School, Wotton-Under-Edge

DEATH

A long time ago, a girl called Lulu went up to the attic to get something and she went through the door. The door closed behind her. Then the lights turned off. She felt very scared. She went into the corner of the attic and a gramophone was playing some music. A ghost came out of the gramophone and... "Boo!"
Lulu screamed really loudly and then she realised that it was her great-grandma and her great-grandma said, "Look at me, you and me are the same! Goodbye."
"Wait, no! Don't go!" said Lulu...

Molly Eliza Donaghey (8)
Blue Coat CE Primary School, Wotton-Under-Edge

THE CROOKED SHIP

In the midst of darkness, there stood Zombella, glaring at Danny. She had three googly, red eyes that could track down her prey. She swivelled left and then right until she balanced on all four feet next to an abandoned ship.
In the distance, Danny heard whispering voices coming from deep down at the very bottom of the crooked ship. With a blink of Danny's eye, he peeked through the frosted glass window. Danny got caught and he was snatched by Zombella! Danny was never seen again in Willington Town. It was in all the newspapers.

Henrietta Arkell (10)
Blue Coat CE Primary School, Wotton-Under-Edge

THE HOUSE NEXT DOOR

Nyla was moving house, she was so excited. Her mum packed lots of boxes, ready and prepared. She also made a delicious cake for their new next-door neighbours. Nyla glanced up at the roof and took a deep breath before knocking on the door. *Rat-a-tat-tat* went the door. The door creaked open by itself. Nyla walked in and shouted, "Hello?"
Bang! The door slammed shut. Her heart was racing. With all her might, she tried to open the door, but nothing. She heard footsteps and Nyla disappeared, just like that!

Scarlett Warren (8)
Blue Coat CE Primary School, Wotton-Under-Edge

THE POTION

On a normal day in a normal town, there lived a girl called Rosie. She was walking into town to get some fresh air when suddenly, she heard a knocking noise in the potion shop next to her. She was intrigued.
On entering the shop, she realised there was only an empty potion bottle in there. That was strange. The label had the words 'Shadow of Darkness' on it. She turned around and saw a figure behind her. She was worried and said, "Oh no! I spilt the potion!"
But then there was no one there. What was it?

Alexandra Yeoman (8)
Blue Coat CE Primary School, Wotton-Under-Edge

THE DEATHSTALKER

I was in bed when it happened. It was the middle of the night, moonlit and terrifying, when I woke up, sweating all over. I tried to get back to sleep. I heard a noise - a creaking of floorboards. I had heard of a walking hand, disembodied from an arm, in horror movies, but that was just a film called Deathstalker. Surely the Deathstalker couldn't be real could it? I watched the place the noise had come from, certain the Deathstalker would jump out and strangle me. I looked. It couldn't be... No! It was my fluffy cat, Max!

Elias Orton (8)

Blue Coat CE Primary School, Wotton-Under-Edge

THE TOYSHOP ON BAKER STREET

It started on Baker Street in an abandoned toyshop with dolls just lying there. When nobody was watching, the door slowly creaked open. *Creeeaaakk!* The dolls awoke and began moving as if they were soldiers. They started to tell their story... it dated back over 100 years. It was as if they had gone through a time machine. They were in the same building, just 100 years before. One candle lit up the gloomy space; it was positioned on a desk. Next to it lay a note and it read, 'Run, fast!'...

Bethany Yeoman (10)
Blue Coat CE Primary School, Wotton-Under-Edge

THE MOVING DOLL

In my room, there was a doll that I got from my grandma who'd died a year ago. It had silky, brown, wavy hair and eyes that shimmered pale silver like the moon. She was dressed in a magenta dress with a pattern of ditsy pink roses and dainty silver shoes. But there was a problem. Every night, she moved around to a new position and I woke up hearing whispers and wails and the scraping of porcelain as she walked along.
Once, I awoke to it moving, but I realised someone was moving it. It was my sister!
"Alice!"

Caitlin Hopkins (10)
Blue Coat CE Primary School, Wotton-Under-Edge

NOT MY BODY

I woke up, but not in my room. I looked very different and I was in a place I had never seen before! I went to school with the thought in my head, *who am I?* I asked my friends, but they all said, "Sam? Who's Sam?"
Throughout the day, I started to lose control of my body. When I got home, my body brutally murdered my parents! I finally got out of my body and possessed a mannequin and become incorporeal. I slept that night and my body, knife in my hand, murdered me with no hesitation or reaction...

Sam Oliver (10)

Blue Coat CE Primary School, Wotton-Under-Edge

THE EVIL BANANA

Once upon a time, there was an evil banana and the banana wanted to escape the house and hunt everybody in the town and beyond. Outside the house, some children called Lyra, Phoebe and Molly were so tempted to go inside and search the house.
The children went in and the banana got out! The children found themselves in a great big room with a table and a fruit bowl. In the fruit bowl was an apple. A head poked out and it really scared the children. The children ran outside and lived, squishing the banana!

Lyra Jean King (7)
Blue Coat CE Primary School, Wotton-Under-Edge

THE STORMY NIGHT

One cold, stormy night in Wotton-under-Edge, a killer unicorn and a zombie rose out of their graves. At the same time, a girl called Lilly was riding her unicorn, doing mounted archery without knowing they were in the same field. When Lilly shot an arrow, there was a scream. A battle for the day went on.
When the farmer came back, there was blood and bones lying in his field. That was the last time someone went there. But this wasn't so long ago. You could see the zombie and the killer unicorn too...

Flo Hall-Smith (8)
Blue Coat CE Primary School, Wotton-Under-Edge

SOMETHING LURKING

Peering out at the abandoned graveyard, I noticed a figure emerge from the shadows. What was this person doing? The moon was barely a sliver of white in the night sky. A faint whisper echoed around me. Something felt wrong.

Crouching in my hiding space, I didn't dare to look. A gasp of air came and an ear-splitting scream dragged me away from my hiding place. I could smell something burning - human flesh. My heart skipped a beat and shivers went down my spine. All that was left was a pile of ashes...

Emma Hunt (11)

Blue Coat CE Primary School, Wotton-Under-Edge

FLAMES

Every night, Mia dreamed of flames burning her room. The nightmare scared her so much, she had a fear of fire. One night, during the terrible nightmare, Mia awoke only to see blazing fire crawling up her walls and a pool of flames swallowing the floor! She couldn't open her mouth to scream. Mia tried to calm herself down, convinced it was only a harmless dream. It was anything but that. The fire crackled, screeches echoed in her mind. Mia never woke up again as she was stolen by the flames.

Abigail Shearer (11)
Blue Coat CE Primary School, Wotton-Under-Edge

THE MURDERER'S CAT

I, Jeff, crept silently through the dimly lit forest at midnight; my master tailed me like a soft-footed bear. I wasn't a bad cat, but my master insisted that I helped him with his crimes. We were off to steal the Crown Jewels of England tonight. My fur bristled as we got closer and closer to the palace. I had a plan to stop my master from his evil crimes.
As soon as he had slipped into the Crown's house, I woke the guards. We shot up the steps and he was arrested. Ha ha to him!

Patrick Dinnis (10)
Blue Coat CE Primary School, Wotton-Under-Edge

THE HAUNTED HOUSE

A boy called Sam had two baby brothers. They were good. Sam was six and his brothers were called Bobby and Stewart. The baby called Stewart wanted to go home. So they went home. Sam was put to bed and Stewart and Bobby went to bed too. Tired, Mum went to bed and so did tired Dad. Then Dad screamed and Mum screamed too. Blood had made them scream! A ghost was in the cellar. They all screamed and ran out of the house. The ghost begged for water. He had some and then disappeared fast!

Clarissa Atkinson (8) & Daisy Hanney (7)
Blue Coat CE Primary School, Wotton-Under-Edge

THE ZOMBIE PARK

It was the dead of night and Ali was about to sneak out to the zombie park. She had heard many tales about how much fun it was during the night.
When she arrived, Ali shivered at the sight of the gates of the zombie park.
Suddenly, they creaked open, welcoming her in.
Bang! Crash! Zombies appeared out of nowhere and started dragging their bodies towards her! Ali turned around and started running for her life, but she couldn't. Ali was closed in and she had nowhere to run. Slowly but surely, the zombies circled around her and ate Ali!

Evie Mae Wilkins (10)
East Wichel Community Primary School & Nursery, Wichelstowe

THE GOBLIN GRANDMA

Deep in the forest, Raghav was lost. He had gone to see his grandma, but couldn't find her house. He had sleek black hair and deep brown eyes. Suddenly, he heard a noise. It sounded like a scream. The boy followed the sound and found a rotting shack. He opened the door and crept inside. Blood splattered the walls. He realised it was his grandma's house. Instantly, a green hand tapped his shoulder. He turned. There was a grubby goblin with a club behind him! It pinned him to the floor with a grotesque hand and said, "Hello Grandson!"

Jonah Teague (10)
East Wichel Community Primary School & Nursery, Wichelstowe

THE CREATURE LURKING FOR DEATH!

It was a peaceful night. A little mouse was scuttling across the floor. A figure approached, it was glaring at the mouse. It was hairy, wrinkly and angry. The monster had a head made of eyeballs! There was a knock on the door. "Ah, I have little guests!" said the creature.

"Trick or treat!" said the children.

The mouse didn't know it was Halloween. The creature let them in and lowered them into a room. There was a squashing machine. He heard a crunch, it was too late for the mouse to save them. "Ha!"

Alice Sibley (9)

East Wichel Community Primary School & Nursery, Wichelstowe

A HALLOWEEN NIGHT IS NEVER NORMAL

It was Halloween night and I was lurking around my home city when, all of a sudden, I stumbled over a zombie's arm. It pulled me into the darkness. "Help! Help!" I shouted.
When I woke up, I was no longer in the graveyard, I was in a dark room. In the distance, I could see a faint outline of some type of monster. "Hello? Is anyone there?" I said in a petrified voice.
Coming out of the darkness were three eerie monsters - a zombie, a werewolf and a vampire. All of a sudden, I was home! That was terrifying!

Betty Peuvrel-Scannell (9)
East Wichel Community Primary School & Nursery, Wichelstowe

HEADS

It was the dead of night, there was a grumpy old man living in a rickety, old caravan in an abandoned forest. He was watching TV when suddenly, the signal went, then went back to normal. Suddenly, he felt a pain in his shoulder. He looked around and there was a white tentacle coming from the door's window and, just above, was a dark head with blood pouring out of its eyes!
The man opened his mouth in astonishment then, two seconds later, all went dark.
Years later, a young boy found the man's head on the floor...

Logan Taylor (11)
East Wichel Community Primary School & Nursery, Wichelstowe

THE ZOMBIES IN THE GRAVEYARD

Suddenly, in the dead of night in the graveyard, a zombie was walking around the misty graveyard, looking for someone or something. Where it had come from? No one knew. Blood poured out of its mouth as it walked. Then it came into the city, eating rats it'd found in dirty drains, drinking the revolting water. The next night in the graveyard, all the zombies came out of their coffins. As they appeared in the night, they walked, unstable on the rusty floor. Rats peeked out and a zombie reached for a girl in the darkness...

Munawwar Abolaji Afolabi (9)
East Wichel Community Primary School & Nursery, Wichelstowe

DARKNESS

Tossing and turning, I felt my eyes grow heavy and my body grow limp. I let out a small moan as I lifted my head from the uncomfortable position it was once in. As I did so, there was a vibration under the bed. I lay there. A shiver ran down my spine. The moaning continued louder. I cupped my hands over my ears.
A long, bony hand grabbed my ankle. Its sharp, dagger-like nails peeled my skin, making blood trickle down my leg. The beast dragged me off my bed. The door handle turned and sunlight killed the darkness...

Kiara Reynolds (11)
East Wichel Community Primary School & Nursery, Wichelstowe

DON'T BREATHE

There was a pink bed with pink pillows and a pink duvet. This girl loved pink. She played with her dolls with pink dresses and wavy hair. She played happily until she heard whispering voices. The girl closed her pale blue eyes and, when she opened them, she was in a blank room. "Hello?" she called out.
Voices were getting louder. They were getting so loud! The girl was finding it hard to breathe. Suddenly, she woke up. Was it all a dream? She went to the bathroom to look in the mirror. She had no head...

Kaiya Wyness (10)
East Wichel Community Primary School & Nursery, Wichelstowe

CREATURES UNDER THE BED

The last thing I remember is falling asleep and waking up again to hear a noise under my bed. I peer into the unknown. An arm reaches out to touch my face and I hide under the covers in fright. Unexpectedly, the creature drags its legs out into the open. The mysterious creature climbs on top of me. I scream, but the creature sticks its finger in my ear. The pain is intolerable.
As I begin to open my eyes, I realise that it's just a dream. I hear a groan under the bed. It's the terrible monster...

Sanshya Sesetty (11)
East Wichel Community Primary School & Nursery, Wichelstowe

THE DRAGON

On a Halloween night in a house, Pika heard a noise. As he wandered down into the hideous basement, his nut-brown hair got in the way of his pale face and sky-blue eyes. When he moved his fringe, he could make out some green scales. A ball of fire hit the step he was about to step on. He could only make out a slight dragon - Nightfury! As he drew closer to the dragon, he felt like he was roasting. As soon as possible, he tried to run. But the dragon's claws cut through Pika's skin. He was dead.

Isabel Catherine Hogg (10)
East Wichel Community Primary School & Nursery, Wichelstowe

THE LAZARI

A little girl lived in an abandoned house. One day, she had a hallucination about a demon girl called the Lazari following her. That night, she went to the basement to check for her cat, but she was not alone. The Lazari tapped her shoulder. She fell back and hit her head on the wall. She passed out and the Lazari took Izzy to the forest to be eaten by wolves!
To this day, the Lazari still lives in the house Izzy lived in. Whoever dares to go into that house will be attacked by a pack of wolves!

Naiyah Irving (8)
East Wichel Community Primary School & Nursery, Wichelstowe

THE HOUSE KNOCK

Santa had heard stories about an underwater house, scary stories. The scary house had lots of spiders and bats. Santa started looking around. The deep, dark water stared, foreboding. What would happen next? He wondered if he should be going to the scary house. He waited and waited.
Sometime later, he thought he heard a knock. The house screamed at him. The chill shook his bones. Nothing happened. Had he imagined it? Another knock, this time louder. "Who's there?" he shrieked.
The house erupted with noise and rocking.
Early the next morning, Santa lay in the water...

Montana Lyn Quarterman (8)
Newlyn School, Newlyn

THE SPOOKY LANE

Charlie had heard spooky stories about a burned old house, scary stories. Charlie sneaked into the spooky house, but someone was in there. Charlie saw a creepy zombie and shouted really loudly, "Who's there?"
Charlie was terrified. A spooky zombie was outside in the lane. Charlie walked back down the spookiest lane near his house and counted all the creepy zombies, so if they came near his house, he'd know how many were left. If they got into this house, he could just kill them with a sword and chop them into pieces!

Harvey Scott Goldsworthy (8)
Newlyn School, Newlyn

THE ABANDONED SCHOOL

Tom had heard stories about an abandoned school, scary ones. He'd been homeless for quite a while now. As the floorboards groaned at him, he thought it was a sign of danger! Tom crept outside slowly and heard a stick break.
"Where are you? I'm not scared. If I run, will you kill me?"
Dashing away, he shivered. He spotted a piece of sweetcorn and a shed. He climbed to the top of the shed and spotted a werewolf! Tom hung the sweetcorn down. Next, he lured the werewolf into the shed. He shut the door and locked it in!

Logan Jax Halliday (8)

Newlyn School, Newlyn

THE ABANDONED MANOR

Jack had heard horrifying stories about the abandoned house. He'd heard that whoever went there would be rich! The darkness of the night led him to the very spooky manor. He knocked, but no one answered. He went in. The house groaned at him. There was the treasure! He dashed for the chest. He threw a rock at it and it faded away. He reached for the door, it was locked. "Help!" he screeched.
Just then, he faded into the wall and was never seen again. The only thing left was some crunched up bones and a pair of shoes...

Freddie Somerset Lane (9)
Newlyn School, Newlyn

THE SPOOKY HOUSE

Sam had heard the stories about the horrible house. She didn't know if she wanted to go there, but she did. She got there at night-time. It was spooky. There was the haunted house. She was in Zombie World and she was scared. She saw so many zombies. There was a big one!
As she was walking to the abandoned house, she heard a knock on the door. She waited and waited for a minute. She was scared but tried the door. "I'm so mad, I want to go in. The abandoned house is locked!"

Tia Darnell (8)

Newlyn School, Newlyn

DAVID'S TRIP

David loved fishing, so he rowed into the lake. He heard the wind howling like a wolf. "Who's there?"
He yelled it again, but louder. He moved to the other side. David felt a cold breeze down his spine. He caught a fish, it was on tight. All of a sudden, it pulled him into the deep water! He was gasping for air. He saw the spiky fish. He'd heard stories about the monsters. David was shocked. They would rise out of the deep water. He was never seen again...

Finley Graham Richards (8)
Newlyn School, Newlyn

WAS IT A DREAM?

Far, far away, somewhere beyond the shadows in a haunted house, lived a vicious vampire, a spooky ghost and a terrifying zombie. It was strange because they didn't have names.
One night, it was Halloween. That meant that the ugly, terrifying zombie and the spooky ghost had to chase trick-or-treaters for the vicious vampire to eat. Some trick-or-treaters ran into the haunted house. The vicious vampire nearly bit one of them!
It turned out that it was all a dream but, as soon as I opened my eyes, vampires, zombies and ghosts surrounded me...

Emily-May Collins (7)
Oasis Academy Long Cross, Lawrence Weston

KILLING VAMPIRES

Once upon a time, there was a haunted house. In the haunted house, there was a vampire family. Before the beautiful sunrise, some scared people went into the haunted house. Suddenly, the door shut on them. Then the vampires came out of hiding. The vampires chased the people! The human kid, called Lily, went to help the others and Lily killed the vampires. Then her parents came and gave Lily a really tight hug. "No one is messing with me!" Lilly said.
"Yes," said her parents. "It will never end!"

Tianna Handley (8)
Oasis Academy Long Cross, Lawrence Weston

THE SCARY VAMPIRE STORY

Around the corner lived a weird vampire in a haunted house. One day, she went to the park, but the horrible and mean zombies came running after her. Unfortunately, it was the spookiest day of her life. She said, "Oh no!"
The vampire ran so quickly. She ran to a haunted house. The vampire entered the house, but then the door locked by itself! She needed to get out by getting an enchanted key on the other side of the room.
She finally got out. You'll never guess what happened next...

Lily-May Walker (7)
Oasis Academy Long Cross, Lawrence Weston

A VAMPIRE AND A HAUNTED HOUSE

Once upon a time, there lived a vampire called Emily. She was scared of almost everything and she was always scared because she lived in a terrifying haunted house.

One day, up on the bumpy ceiling, she saw a spooky attic. Emily got a ladder and climbed into the spooky attic. Vampire Emily thought it was okay, but it wasn't, it was spooky! At that moment, everything started jiggling and shaking and Emily was afraid. It was just her ghost friend, moving all the stuff around! They both got out.

Milly Jay Matthews (7)
Oasis Academy Long Cross, Lawrence Weston

SCARY DREAM

After dusk, in a haunted mansion, there lived a boy called Charlie and he was in bed. Suddenly, he got out of bed and he saw a ghost and tons of potions and, of course, a couple of shadows! As quick as a flash, he went downstairs and went to get some food but, unfortunately, there was no more left. Suddenly, he looked behind him and saw a ghost! He didn't know what to do, but he eventually got away.
After midnight, Charlie's dad woke him up and Charlie realised it was just a dream!

Connor-James Mills (7)
Oasis Academy Long Cross, Lawrence Weston

THE LIFE OF ZOMBIES THAT NEVER ENDS!

Nine years ago, in a spine-chilling haunted house lived a revolting devil and a boneless ghost. They played horrible, evil and spooky games. As quick as a flash, the revolting devil and quick ghost stayed until midnight and then zombies marched towards them in the graveyard. The devil got his golden staff and stabbed 2,000 zombies in 1hr, 20m and 11s. The ghost helped too. In the blink of an eye, the devil went back to the ghost's house, but the army of zombies never ended...

Kian-Day Anthony Middleton (8)
Oasis Academy Long Cross, Lawrence Weston

LOCKED IN

After dusk, I went trick or treating and saw a house, but it was in the woods. It looked haunted. I thought someone was trying to scare me, but no. I walked inside, there were bloody eyeballs staring at me! When I turned around, stuff was moving on its own. I got so scared. I quickly ran to the door, but it was locked! Suddenly, a bloody vampire jumped and the bloody vampire bit me. We both had evil in our eyes.

I got outside, my sister was out there. I bit her...

Grace Rose Pellowe (7)
Oasis Academy Long Cross, Lawrence Weston

THE HAUNTED HOUSE

One mortifying, deadly night, me and my friends were trick or treating. "Let's go home," said Tyler
"Why?" I asked.

Fred replied, "Woah, let's go in that house!"

We all dashed inside because we were being chased by zombies. As we walked inside, we were trapped so Tyler threw his phone, but the phone came right back and knocked him out. I stomped on the floor and fell, but I bounced back up. It was a bouncy castle!

Rhys-Evan Smith (8)
Oasis Academy Long Cross, Lawrence Weston

IN THE GRAVE

Today, I was in a spooky, terrifying, scary house. I was so scared because a ghost appeared. The ghost trapped me in a cage! I tried to get out, but it was so strong, I couldn't get out. Then my mum came to rescue me, but then my mum got trapped as well. Then my dog came to rescue us. He sneaked past the ghost and busted us out. We said, "Thank you. Good boy!"

"Now, let's get out," said Mum.

When we got home, we sat on the sofa.

Riley B (7)

Oasis Academy Long Cross, Lawrence Weston

HAUNTED HALLOWEEN

Once upon a time, there lived an unidentified person who lived in a secret lair. He was always hidden and loved scary things, so the very next day, he went to the eerie graveyard. After midnight, he luckily caught a spine-chilling monster in his line of sight. He looked around and saw a gargantuan radiation machine which would blast the monster to dust. Suddenly, he activated it and the monster was no more and the area looked as dirty as a battlefield!

Ollie Coles (8)

Oasis Academy Long Cross, Lawrence Weston

READ IF YOU DARE

Once upon a time, there lived zombies called Ellie and Lucas. One dark, scary Halloween night, Ellie and Lucas went out for a drive in their Civic to scare children. Suddenly, Lucas found a mansion.
The next morning, Lucas went into the mansion and couldn't get out. Lucas went upstairs and found 1899 chainsaws. Finally, Lucas cut the door open and stole the chainsaws, going home to build his own mansion. The two zombies lived happily ever after.

Lucas Michael Pritchard (8)
Oasis Academy Long Cross, Lawrence Weston

THE HAUNTED HOUSE

Far away, a little girl went to a haunted mansion to trick or treat. The creaky door opened by itself. She felt scared and suddenly, as fast as lightning, someone pushed her inside and the door locked before she could escape!
She felt sleepy, so she slept in a horrible bed and she forgot how she'd got there.
When she woke up, she wondered why she was there...

Millie C (7)
Oasis Academy Long Cross, Lawrence Weston

IN THE CHILLY GRAVEYARD

Once upon a time near the chilly graveyard after midnight, I was going trick or treating. A weird car took me to the chilly graveyard and I was stuck in the middle of nowhere. There were zombies coming out of the mud and out of every grave! I saw my dad pull up and ran to my daddy's amazing car. My daddy was driving the car. We finally got home!

Luke William Rogers (7)
Oasis Academy Long Cross, Lawrence Weston

TRICK OR TREATING MYSTERY

One dark, horrifying night, Charlie and his best friend were out trick or treating. They went at about 9.17pm and they went from house to house, collecting their candy, but one house they went to was strange. They didn't care. When they arrived, before Charlie could see it, his best friend's neck was torn apart! Charlie ran as fast as he could. He made it home in minutes. Before he could go into the safe, warm house, someone took him! The police found out who it was and then sent them to prison. Charlie was safe.

Martin Geberta (8)
Old Sarum Primary School, Old Sarum

THE PUPPET MAN

I tiptoed along the slightly narrowing cobblestone road. I turned my attention to a shop. It was called Puppet. I decided to go inside.
I glanced at the shop owner, who was in black. He whispered something. Suddenly, all the puppets and creepy dolls began to move and sing the same tune, "La la!"
The blinds started to open and close. Was it the wind? I ventured outside to tell someone what was happening. "There's a puppet shop over there!"
"There hasn't been anything there since the 15th century! Now it's a graveyard!"
"What are you talking about?"

Arabella Merrick (10)
St Breock Primary School, Wadebridge

A CUPBOARD AND NOTHING ELSE...

On a bleak, mystical night, an unusual school rose up from the earth. Two little girls, Lizzy and Petra, were standing outside the brown, bone-chilling door. They crept inside and played hide-and-seek. Lizzy finished counting and began her search for Petra. She tiptoed down a narrow corridor and arrived at a metal ladder. She climbed higher than she had ever climbed before. Eventually, Lizzy reached the attic. Standing bare, dusty and ancient, was a cupboard. She ventured into the dirty chamber. She twisted the rusty knob on the cupboard door. Petra was no longer a girl! She'd been transformed...

Maisie Hunt (11)

St Breock Primary School, Wadebridge

THE CLICK

The rain spat upon Stacy's freezing head, she had reached her friend's house. She needed shelter. She knocked on the door. Nothing.
"Mmh," she muttered to herself.
Stacy turned the doorknob... *Smash!* Suddenly, a man appeared. He was in an old, battered hockey mask, ripped jeans and a black hoodie that looked very, very scruffy. He clicked his fingers and suddenly, she was back in her car, driving on the A30! She looked down at her hands. They were transparent! Then she realised she was a frail and cold ghost, trapped forever in a loop of the old man's memories!

Jude Smith (10)
St Breock Primary School, Wadebridge

THE ABANDONED SCHOOL

It wasn't allowed and I knew it. I was curious too. The school had been deserted for a century. In that time, nobody had set foot inside. Nervously, I opened the door and stepped in. The floor was thick with dust, I was grateful for it. It muffled my footsteps.
As I neared the end of the corridor, I heard whispering. I froze. Where were those noises coming from? I stepped forwards to investigate. A floorboard creaked, lightning flashed, illuminating a hooded figure standing in front of me. "You've come at last!" thundered the figure chillingly.
I turned and ran...

Sylvie Carter (10)

St Breock Primary School, Wadebridge

ABBY AND THE CREEPY DOLL

Abby was walking around her estate and saw the horrible, abandoned house. She knew nobody dared go there, but she wanted to.
Abby went right up to the door and knocked.
She didn't expect someone to answer, but she heard footsteps getting louder from the house!
The door opened and a little girl, holding a wooden doll, said, "Hello. Do you want to come in?"
"No thank you!"
Suddenly, the scary little girl moved her finger and it started hammering down with rain. Abby rushed in, then the creepy doll put a spell on Abby. She was cursed forever...

Grace Martin (11)
St Breock Primary School, Wadebridge

THE TERRIFYING ADVENTURE

Timmy finally reached the toy store. He strode in to see a man standing there. Timmy bought a doll. The doll surprisingly came alive! It was a voodoo doll. It said, "Follow me," so he followed the doll.
The voodoo doll took him around the back of the haunted toyshop to a dark man. He led Timmy into the forest. Unexpectedly, Timmy heard a growl. He turned around and there was a werewolf with glowing red eyes and slobber dripping from its jaws!
Suddenly, he woke up, his forehead soaking. It was all a dream. "Phew," said Timmy quietly.

Hatti Du Cros (10)
St Breock Primary School, Wadebridge

THE HOLIDAY OF SCREAMS

As I explored my holiday surroundings, I decided to sit down and relax. Then, without warning, bloodshot eyeballs came shooting down onto my face! I scrambled up, ran and tripped. My heart was thumping. They came tumbling down quicker and quicker. Unfortunately, I couldn't get up. I tugged and heaved my leg, but it just kept sinking. Singing in unison, dolls with missing body parts and hooded figures started to surround me. I was terrified, it was like I was being sucked up or eaten.
A few screams later, I fell through the sand and onto my comfy bed!

Meredith Durston (10)
St Breock Primary School, Wadebridge

MYSTERY AT THE FAIR

He noticed a hooded figure with a mask stood by the side of the road. Pretending it wasn't there, he sang happy birthday to Tom. When they arrived at the fair, they went on the slippery slides, the funhouse and the hall of mirrors. That was when Jack spotted him again. Trying not to ruin the special day, Jack suggested, "Let's go on the roller coaster." Tom agreed. There was an endless queue! Finally, they jumped in a carriage. During the ride, the figure in front turned around. It was him! Strangely, they were never seen ever again...

Katie Hodges (11)
St Breock Primary School, Wadebridge

DRAGON

On a bright sunny day, strolling through the lush forest, I couldn't help notice the hypnotising figure in the sky. Unexpectedly, the sky turned a fiery red. A dragon peered over the deep emerald roof that the trees gave me. The dragon started screeching at the top of its lungs, "Give it back! I need it more than you!" I started wandering around in circles, thinking of what he meant. Searching my pockets, I took out my pocket watch that glistened like a star in the night. The dragon vanished! As he did, he took the pocket watch with him!

Isla Baird (11)
St Breock Primary School, Wadebridge

DARK SHADOWS

Zoe approached the doll shop and ventured through the door. Her first sight was an old dollmaker, sitting in a rocking chair. Next to him sat a wooden doll. "Annabell is her name. Annabell," hollered the man.
Suddenly, a big pack of dolls wandered towards Zoe, singing, "La la la la la," over and over again. Soon, the noise became deafening and strange, so Zoe ran and ran. The pack kept on running towards Zoe like little penguins. Annabell was in front of the pack, singing the loudest of them all. "La la la la la la..."

Evie Rose Callis (10)
St Breock Primary School, Wadebridge

THE NIGHTMARE!

Sam strolled towards the houses covered in decorations for Halloween in his outfit (a zombie). As he arrived at an old house, he saw a floor mat. 'Enter if you dare', it read. He rang the doorbell. There stood an exact replica of him. His outfit! His face! Everything! He looked around, the hairs on his neck stood up as he moved around slowly. Then he noticed lots of grey zombies charging at him. Sam scampered away. They ran up to him. He screamed, then woke up. He heard his mum say softly to him, "Is everything alright dear?"

Winnie Rose Durston (10)

St Breock Primary School, Wadebridge

THE ABANDONED ISLAND

It wasn't allowed! However, he still did it. I told him not to but he continued to do so. I couldn't let him go by himself, so I stayed in the boat. I only saw it briefly and I didn't know what'd happened. We travelled to the theme park on the island. It'd been abandoned sixty-two years ago. It was deserted. Then he disappeared.
I discovered his camera. The pictures were creepy - old costumes and dolls. Finally, there was a picture of darkness with eight glowing eyes. I left, it was too creepy. I never saw him again!

Iona Penington (11)
St Breock Primary School, Wadebridge

THE DOLL AND THE CAT

It was dark. Jack was walking home. He was crossing a bridge when, *bang!* He was pushed against a pole and everything went black. When he came around, he was in a forest, a forbidden forest. In front of him appeared a little box. Inside was something that froze the blood in him. It was a creepy doll, it was looking up at him! Suddenly, he heard a crack behind him. "Who's there?"
Before him approached a cat, his cat. He peered at his feet and then started to run in the direction of the sun. Then he woke up!

Oscar Luxton (11)
St Breock Primary School, Wadebridge

THE LIGHT IN THE DARK

It was the 27th of November 1916. It was getting dark. Shadows crept all around the used army site. I was scared. Out of the silent forest came a flash. "What was that?" I whispered.
"I don't know," answered the sarge.
I decided to venture up the hill. I clambered up towards the light. Then, as if I was in a nightmare, a creepy Santa appeared! I looked into his eyes and it forced me back.
I woke up in the morning and I looked at my watch. It was the day before yesterday!

Laurence Miller (11)
St Breock Primary School, Wadebridge

The Stalker

Crunch! I heard it! I was in a forest, alone. There it was again. I quickly turned and saw it. A man, about eight to ten feet tall, just staring at me! I could not move. I tried to yelp, though nothing came out. I started running, but he chased me!
I woke up. *Phew!* It was all a dream... Then I heard three bangs at the window. I opened the blue velvet curtains to see the same man from my dream! Just like in my dream, he was very tall and was just staring at me... It was Grandad!

Benjamin Carey (10)
St Breock Primary School, Wadebridge

DEAD FIRE

It all started with a cowboy, he was called Fire. He lived in the Wild West. He loved the Wild West and loved horse riding, showdowns and going out alone at midnight. But, when he was going out alone at night on his favourite horse (Blaze), a gigantic purple shockwave struck everyone. Then, without warning, everyone turned into zombies and the Wild West turned into the Dead West! Then Fire was renamed Dead Fire. His clothes were ripped, he had neon green flames radiating from his body and, from that day, the zombie apocalypse obliterated the whole western zombie village!

Andrew Riley Talatala (10)
St Mary's Catholic Primary School, Ryde

THE BURGLAR FOG

Once upon a time, there was a witch shopkeeper. The witch was reading in her bed upstairs at midnight. Suddenly, she heard a loud crashing noise. She scrambled downstairs and looked through the staff door window. There were two burglars in the shop! The witch decided to cast a spell on the burglars. This spell was the anti-burglar fog system. "Igglety, pigglety, higglety hog! Be blinded by my mighty fog!"

Unable to see, the burglars bumped into each other and knocked themselves out. The police arrived and arrested them. The village thought the witch was a hero!

Anna Longley (7)

St Vigor & St John CE Primary School, Chilcompton

WITCHES

Once upon a time, there lived a witch. She was called Winnie. She had long fingers. Once, she wasn't a witch, but another witch had turned her into one. Winnie had messy hair. She once had a beautiful home. Now, inside it was dark and messy. It had cracks in the walls. "It's gross."
One day, Winnie rode her broomstick to get ingredients for her spells to turn herself back into a human. She turned back into a human. "I'm beautiful again! Boys will love me! I've missed being a human." She tidied her house. "Wow! Much better!"

Isabella Steele (7)
St Vigor & St John CE Primary School, Chilcompton

JAZZY AND THE GHOSTLY GHOULS

I woke up and tiptoed downstairs to realise I was in a church. My aunt, Lizz, appeared, asking me how I'd got here. "I woke up from a bad dream and ended up here."
"Oh," replied Lizz. We crept into the kitchen and started cooking. Suddenly, a vampire appeared and growled at us, so we sprinted into the graveyard. Then we saw an evil witch pointing a wand at us, cackling. She said, "I'm going to get you now!"
We ran upstairs into a room where a mirror hung. When we looked into the mirror, we realised we were ghosts...

Grace Cathleen Creamer (7)
St Vigor & St John CE Primary School, Chilcompton

GREEN ZOMBIE APPLE THIEF

In a gloomy street stood a mansion, next door to Peter. Simon walked up the path excitedly to see Peter for a sleepover. That night, they read comics with torches and both fell asleep.
Suddenly, Simon woke to a creaky noise. He got up slowly and went to the window. Outside stood a green zombie picking apples! The zombie looked up at the window. It was a green monstrous beast with red eyes. Simon hid under his duvet, frozen in fear until morning.
The boys went downstairs for breakfast. Mum had made apple pie. Was Peter's mum the mysterious zombie?

Liam Marden (7)
St Vigor & St John CE Primary School, Chilcompton

THE PLANE CRASH

Alix and a few of his friends were riding in a plane over the never-ending rainforest. Suddenly, they felt the plane going down, down, down until... *boom!* They hit the mysteriously smoky ground and Alix fell out. When he did so, he cut his knee open. You could see the bleeding down his ragged jeans. He went back to the plane, but there was a dark force field. His friends were in there, terrified and absolutely traumatised. He felt something on his shoulder. It was green and slimy. He reached for the handle, but the force field froze him...

Zachary Cardy (8)
St Vigor & St John CE Primary School, Chilcompton

THE MYSTERY OF JACK

Once upon a time, there was a boy called Jack. One day, Jack and his friends went to the top of a hill and found a strange-looking house. Jack's friends dared him to go in, so he did. Suddenly, the door slammed behind him! It wasn't his friends. Jack jumped and tried to open the door, but it was locked! Jack's friends shouted through the window. Jack listened to them and turned around but then he disappeared. Jack's friends opened the door and searched for Jack, but only found a picture of him. Nobody knew what'd happened to him...

Dean James Cross (7)
St Vigor & St John CE Primary School, Chilcompton

TRICK OR TREAT?

I nervously ring the doorbell. Will it be a trick or a treat this time? Suddenly, the huge door creaks slowly open as if by magic! "Hello, is anyone there?" I whisper.
I summon up the courage to poke my head around to take a closer look. Nobody is there, but I spy a trail of sweets that leads to a gloomy cupboard. I can't resist the temptation, so I go inside. Terrifying noises surround me. I quickly feel for a light switch but, before I find it, the light turns on by itself! "Surprise! Happy Halloween!" shout my family.

Rosie Mullan (8)
St Vigor & St John CE Primary School, Chilcompton

MONSTER CREW

The Meany Taila was going down fast. Everybody was running to the back and the last lifeboat was launched. Suddenly, something happened... The ship was under the water and everybody turned into monsters! The monster crew was gathering up for a talk and then they started to stop the boat. While the monsters were busy stopping the boat, some divers were looking at the ship. Then they heard screams of terror. They screamed in fear and then the ship shot into the sky! All the monsters turned back into humans and called the ship the Harri Taila.

Harri Ford (8)

St Vigor & St John CE Primary School, Chilcompton

THE STRANGE CHARLIE BROWN

I heard whispers at the front door with a knock. An unfamiliar voice appeared. "Hi, I'm Charlie Brown. Can you help me find my dog, please?" "Yes," I said. I followed him out into the pitch-black night. Bats flew over our heads, branches broke under our feet, owls howled. We stood in a graveyard. I looked at the stone that was in front of me. It said, 'Charlie Brown'.
In shock, I turned around and Charlie Brown was gone! I sprinted to my house and the door slowly opened. Suddenly, I woke up screaming...

Rose Laura Gierlicka (7)
St Vigor & St John CE Primary School, Chilcompton

ZELLE THE ZOMBIE!

Once there lived a zombie called Zelle and a girl called Lucy. Lucy lived in a hotel type of house. Zelle lived in an ancient wooden hut with spider legs.
One day, Lucy got extremely bored, so she shuffled into the woods to feel better. Suddenly, Lucy came face-to-face with the ancient wooden hut. Lucy got so petrified, she screamed. But she felt brave, so she went in. Inside, it was abandoned and it was falling to pieces. On a shelf, there were some potions. On the floor was blood. She turned around and spotted the green zombie...

Darcy Marion Cole (7)
St Vigor & St John CE Primary School, Chilcompton

Revenge Of Currysauce

Once upon a time, on a late afternoon, a chip shop owner threw out some curry sauce. He made a mistake because it landed in a radioactive puddle and turned into a huge, radioactive, giant monster! It named itself Lord Currysauce and set off for London where his arch-enemy (Lord Mushy Peas) lived. He stomped on every village he came across. Finally, he got to London where Lord Mushy Peas lived. Lord Mushy Peas met Lord Currysauce and they had a huge battle. But it went on and on and on. Finally, Lord Mushy Peas killed Lord Currysauce!

Jack Egerton (8)
St Vigor & St John CE Primary School, Chilcompton

JIM AND THE HAUNTED HOUSE

It was a dark and gloomy house. People never went in because they never came out. Jim was sure there was some treasure inside. He opened the door and walked in. The floorboards creaked and the wallpaper was peeling. Something moved. Something touched him on the shoulder. Jim turned and saw a zombie! The zombie dragged him to the cellar and locked the door. Jim pushed the wall and found a secret passage. He was in a different room now. On a shelf was a box of coins. Treasure! Jim took the coins and ran home.

Arthur Raphael Clifton Mills (8)
St Vigor & St John CE Primary School, Chilcompton

VOICES

In the spooky darkness around me, I could hear voices. I walked towards them but, as I switched the light on, they disappeared. I looked in the other room, it seemed pretty quiet in this room. I went into another room. As I went into the room, I saw a blue flash. I looked into the corner and something vanished! When I looked at the ceiling, I found a blue monster hiding in the shadows above me. It fell from the ceiling and broke the floorboards. I ran after it and saw it definitely was a blue monster!

Harry Robinson (7)
St Vigor & St John CE Primary School, Chilcompton

THE ZOMBIE PRINCESS

Once upon a time, there was a zombie princess. She was in a huge cave with blood and grime on the walls. She was locked up in the cave. She was guarded by a fierce, incredible, huge troll that wore a mossy cloak. He would never let the zombie princess out into the world.

One day, she heard a zombie coming to eat her brain but actually, he was coming to rescue her! The troll woke up and ate him. There was lots of blood. Then someone came and stabbed the troll and saved the zombie princess!

Jessica Joanne Book (7)
St Vigor & St John CE Primary School, Chilcompton

THE REVENGE OF THE TREE

Once there was a gang who said, "I dare you to go into the cemetery and stab a knife in a tree."

A boy said, "I will."

So, in the middle of the night, he crept into the haunted cemetery, feeling terrified and scared. He quickly stuck the knife into the tree, but he also put the knife through his jumper and the tree! A dark shadow fell upon him and a green branch grabbed him and lifted him onto the tallest branch. It took all night to climb down and escape!

Nico Coghlan (8)

St Vigor & St John CE Primary School, Chilcompton

A NIGHTMARE?

In a faraway place was a girl called Matilda. She lived in a haunted house. On her front door was a skull! Matilda had an unusual dad. He had two sharp, pointy teeth and only wore black.
One night, she awoke to a strange noise. As she crept out of bed, she saw a bat fly past. She was so surprised that she jumped out of her skin and screamed. *What's that?* she thought. In the hallway, she saw a dark figure. To her surprise, it was her dad. Was her dad a real vampire?

Amy Niamh Skivington (7)
St Vigor & St John CE Primary School, Chilcompton

I'M KRYSTAL

I'm Krystal. My dream haunted me until I turned twenty-one, the day I died.
In the dream, it was a bitter night when a faceless man appeared (no facial features, not even the hint of a nose). He knelt beside me with a blood-covered knife. Here, I would wake up covered in beads of sweat, shaking. This was how it went every night, until my twenty-first birthday.
The party was like any other: friends, family, presents and party poppers. Then the dream came, like always, but I was awake and he was there, so close I could hear him wheezing...

Ada Lowrie (9)
Stroud Valley Community School, Stroud

CRIMSON, MY LEAST FAVOURITE COLOUR

Crimson has been my least favourite colour since Mum died. We weren't even going that fast. The Roller hit; the airbag failed. The shockwave was like the thud of a bass speaker. Mum flew out of the windscreen and lay there on the road. After that chrome Rolls Royce hit her, the driver in his crimson suit just got out and shouted some words. I don't know what he said. The world just went silent for me and I stood there, a tsunami of tears rolling down my face. I stared at him until his body became translucent and disappeared...

Theo Johnson (10)
Stroud Valley Community School, Stroud

THE WALLS

The girl slept for hours. When she awoke, she found herself in a dark, dank room. Her wheezy breathing echoed against the crumbling walls. Sitting up, she rubbed her eyes. Trying to find her bearings, she tripped and scraped her elbow on the hard ground. Cold blood dripped down her arm. Standing up, she felt for the walls. They began to vibrate, the room closing in on her. As the girl felt her life disappearing, she saw a tiny crack of light slip into view, but by the time she'd thought she could make it, it was too late...

Esther Wardle (11)
Stroud Valley Community School, Stroud

A HALLOWEEN FRIGHT

It was Halloween. I was dressed as a vampire with a bloodstained shirt and yellow fangs. It was the perfect kind of night. Everything was caked in darkness. The stars splattered the midnight sky like pale blood. I was walking up an alleyway when I heard it. *Chomp! Chomp!* All I could see was a mound of white cloth piled up on a doorstep just metres away. Slowly, I tiptoed towards the pile. I realised that it was floating, actually hovering above the ground just like a real ghost! It couldn't be, could it?

Rose Sinclair (9)
Stroud Valley Community School, Stroud

THE PARTY ON HALLOWEEN

Once upon a time, there was a girl called Lucy. It was her birthday and she went trick or treating. She met up with some friends and they all went to a house to knock on the door. Out came an old lady who didn't give them any sweets. She did give them a fright! Lucy was left alone. The old lady grabbed her. As quick as a flash, Lucy put the old lady in the oven because she was a witch! When Lucy got out of the witch's house, she told her mummy about killing the witch!

Louisa Lavan (6)

Wardour Catholic Primary School, Tisbury

THE ONE-LEGGED WITCH

There once was a boy who was locked in a cellar with nothing to eat. Suddenly, a spooky witch appeared. The boy was terrified of the witch because she was cackling and only had one leg. He ran through the wine cellar until he escaped.
On the way, he met a gang of witches. The boss demanded to turn him into a mouse, but he ran away. He ran for two hours until he got to Grandma's.
When he got there, he had food and played on the swing and played planes and cars.

Ralph Master (6)
Wardour Catholic Primary School, Tisbury

MONSTER TOWN

Once upon a time, I was walking by an abandoned church when the ground started to rumble. Zombies started launching out of the ground! They chased after me, some tripped over gravestones and some fell into graves and smashed in half. I pushed some over. I lost them.

I then found a haunted house. I went inside. *Creak* went the floorboards, *screech* went the walls, *thump, thump, thump* went the giant footsteps of a monster walking right towards me! "Argh!" I screamed.

"Argh!" growled the monster.

It launched at me. I could hear my own death coming...

Thomas Weeks (7)

Yeo Moor Primary School, Clevedon

MONSTER'S MEAL

Midnight found a 1,000-year-old school at night. Shielding her face from the hailstones hitting her like icicles, she slowly crept inside, opening the wrecked door that creaked like joints on a skeleton's hand. Pushing away cobwebs, a spider scuttled across her hand, making her shudder. Suddenly, a shriek sounded from down the damp, dark, cave-like corridor. She crept down the corridor to where she'd heard the scream. A clatter came from one of the classrooms. Pushing open the door, she was hit by the stench of rotten flesh. Suddenly, the door slammed shut behind her with a loud bang...

Summer Phoenix Christie (7)
Yeo Moor Primary School, Clevedon

The Ghoul Of Asovert Graveyard

A grey squirrel clambered onto the branch above me and a nut fell on my friend's head. My other friend, Ivy, ran towards Nathan but vanished in her stride. Me and Nathan jumped back in astonishment. Nathan's green hat lifted and slapped Nathan in the face. He vanished, so did his hat. A vicious fog rolled in and dangerous cackles echoed through the graveyard. A grotesque smell spread from a grave dug yesterday. The creepy gravestone toppled backwards and the earth under me rose. A pale hand reached from the ground. The eerie, bone-chilling hand unearthed its own disgusting body...

Jake Gurney (8)
Yeo Moor Primary School, Clevedon

THE MYSTERIOUS GRAVEYARD

Once upon a time, there were some young boys walking down an alley like zombies. They saw a creepy, broken graveyard. After a few minutes, one said, "Let's go in."

"Okay."

Then they saw a broken skeleton body and said, "Ew!"

Suddenly, they saw a hairy wolf with giant, red, bulging eyes. He said, "I'm going to put you in a swimming pool of snot, poop, brains and skulls!"

"No!" they said.

He picked up the two boys and then sucked some of their blood. Next, he threw them in the pool. They never returned...

Florence Hampton (7)

Yeo Moor Primary School, Clevedon

THE SPOOKY MANSION

On a dark and mysterious night, a boy called Kester saw an abandoned, old, rotting mansion. Kester decided to tiptoe up to it. Some thick fog rolled in unexpectedly. Kester was just about to open the door, but it just opened. It was a bit creepy. Looking behind himself all the time, Kester crept past every door, but one door had creepy music. Someone was in there!

Kester opened the door. It was someone with a mask on. It was Project Zorgo! "Argh!" Kester screamed.

It was his grandad. Kester told his parents, but they didn't believe him.

Jake Hayes (8)
Yeo Moor Primary School, Clevedon

THE WEREWOLF...

She stepped into the mansion. "Argh!" screamed Ellie in terror.
It was the soft tongue from a cute werewolf! She was very surprised and went inside the haunted mansion with the werewolf. It was a dark and creepy place with pictures on the walls. They went upstairs with a frightened look on their faces. In a room, there were red eyes. They walked further into the room. It was a bloodthirsty vampire! Ellie and the werewolf ran down the stairs; the door was locked. She went into the kitchen, opened the window and ran away, never to be seen again.

Mymoonah Sorowar (7)
Yeo Moor Primary School, Clevedon

ZOMBIE

One late night, two little children were going trick or treating. Their names were Ray and Morgan. Ray and Morgan found an abandoned school, they were petrified. They crept up to it. Suddenly, a knife dropped and hit Morgan's hands. Morgan got sucked into the school. Ray gasped. "I've got to get her!"
Ray sneaked in and saw blood on the walls. He heard a girl scream. Ray thought it was Morgan. A zombie was trying to eat her brain! She was banging on the door, but he couldn't free her. Ray ran home, scared, and left Morgan for dead.

Morgan Jones (7)
Yeo Moor Primary School, Clevedon

THE HALLOWEEN NIGHT

It was late at night on Halloween when Jason was trick or treating. While he was walking, he saw the remains of a house that had burnt down 100 years ago. He decided to knock on it anyway. An old lady opened the door. Jason was about to run back home, but the lady smirked and said, "Do you want some cake?"
"Yes please!"
Walking in, he was suddenly trapped and the lady gave him guts and blood! "Mwahaha!" cackled the old woman. "If you don't eat this, I will kill you!"
He quickly gulped it down...

Ahnaf M W Sheikh (8)
Yeo Moor Primary School, Clevedon

THE FORBIDDEN HOSPITAL

One gloomy day, a little boy called Leno found himself by an abandoned hospital. He gently tiptoed across the half-broken floor, surrounded by dead mummies. He knocked loudly but nobody answered. He had no choice but to enter. A shiver ran down his body as he saw wooden stairs leading into the dark. Suddenly, he felt the floorboards give way and he was falling, falling...
Around him, he saw thousands of zombies. He pushed through the terrifying creatures to the exit. He found himself by the forbidden hospital door and he ran straight home to bed.

Charlie Oliver Parker (8)
Yeo Moor Primary School, Clevedon

MYSTERIOUS HOSPITAL!

I walked into an abandoned hospital and I walked into a room with my little sister. It was 3am on Friday the 13th. The room we walked into had something sat on the bed. It was a doll... Chucky! Suddenly, he turned his head and looked at me. He said, "Do you want to play?"
I was petrified, the doll had a knife! Then suddenly, Jason stomped in and roared, "Let's go camping! Hahahaha!"
Then blood started to drip onto the floor. Suddenly, the floor started to crack and lots of zombies started to climb out of the crack...

Isla Stephens (8)
Yeo Moor Primary School, Clevedon

THE SCARIEST STORY EVER

It was late at night on Halloween. A boy called Ray and a girl called Morgan were walking in the woods until they found a 100-year-old abandoned school. They decided to go inside, so they did. Then the door slammed shut. Ray and Morgan were very afraid. Suddenly, they saw a Frankenstein. He was running at them! They tried to escape, but the exit was full of giant tarantulas. They couldn't escape! There was nowhere to run. They were now surrounded by two Frankensteins! The most terrifying thing was that the Frankensteins' pet was there too...

Ray Payne (8)
Yeo Moor Primary School, Clevedon

THE BLACK DUST

One dusty, cold night, a little boy called Bobby went out with his friends. Then Bobby found a little floating chimney. Suddenly, he teleported to a cold house. *Wait? There's a door?* Then he heard a laugh and a creak. A cauldron appeared out of nowhere and lots of potions started to float, but they hadn't been there before. A cold pile of dust came from the chimney that Bobby'd come from. It slowly went towards him and he turned on the light. It was just his dad playing games on Halloween night! His dad was very good at scaring!

Taylor Riggs (8)
Yeo Moor Primary School, Clevedon

DEATH IS HERE

On a spooky Halloween night, there was a man on his bike. When he woke up, he saw Baldy. Baldy dragged him into a horrid mansion. There were demons guarding the grimy door and the windows were smashed. Dragons flew in mid-air. There were scratches on the doors made by werewolves. Living in the mansion were killer clowns and Five Nights At Freddy's people. Spiders hung from every corner of the mansion and dragons breathing fire could be heard around the foggy graveyard. It was the spookiest night you'd ever have. Suddenly, the man woke up...

Ethan Huxtable (8)
Yeo Moor Primary School, Clevedon

THE HAUNTED ATTIC!

The attic in my house was scary. I didn't know why it was, but it was, so I never went up there. Once, in the horrible and dusty attic, there were zombies hanging upside down, drizzling blood from their mouths. There were deadly spiders with creepy red eyes. There were ghosts in there too.

In the night, I heard whispers. *Crash!* I heard the glass break from the terrifying wind. I saw a shadow, a figure moving all on its own. I was terrified. I heard two footsteps and... It was Mum and Dad. "How did you get up here?"

Emmanuel Manoj (8)
Yeo Moor Primary School, Clevedon

ALEX AND THE PETRIFYING SKINLESS WOLVES

One dark night, a little boy called Alex went to an abandoned school. He walked into every classroom. It said 'They're coming' on the walls in blood. Alex was worried as he tried to open the exit door. It was locked! Something moved in a room. He checked the room, there was a pack of skinless wolves!
They chased him all around the school. He found a sharp knife and stabbed the skinless wolves. One had a key. He took the key and unlocked the exit door. Finally, he'd made it home alive! He told his mum what had happened.

Xander Batt (8)
Yeo Moor Primary School, Clevedon

TAYLOR'S NIGHT IN THE GRAVEYARD

There once lived a boy called Taylor. His dad took him to a graveyard. Taylor ran off and got lost. It started to get dark. Taylor heard growls and then zombies started to crawl out the ground. Taylor ran, but they kept coming! He started to fight them. They were too strong. He ran and ran. Everywhere Taylor looked, there were zombies. The walls were too tall to climb. He was trapped! There was no way out. Taylor kept fighting, they'd ripped his clothes and had smelly, rotten skin. It started to get light and the smelly zombies burned!

Joseph Arnold (8)
Yeo Moor Primary School, Clevedon

HARRY POTTER AND THE CAVE

Harry escaped from his mansion and chased the full moon to a dimly lit cave. He held his wand out and made a blue glow. Out of nowhere, a rock fell, blocking the doorway. Fourteen-year-old Harry was dragged from the hard floor and got thrown to the back of the cave. A vampire was ready to drink Harry's blood. "Accio vampire!" yelled Harry with a plan to run out of the cave.
Luckily, the vampire was stuck to the roof! Harry ran to the sunlight and the vampire followed him. Gleeful, Harry saw the vampire burn to death!

Delylah Waller (8)
Yeo Moor Primary School, Clevedon

THE DAWN RAILWAY!

It was dawn. I was walking towards this strange place. At first, I thought it was a swimming pool. As I continued, it looked like a railway, then I got further. I guessed I was right, it was a railway.
When I got inside, I heard a sound around the corner. I saw a pond, but it wasn't that. It sounded like, 'Mama' and there it was again! "Mama," it continued but it didn't stop me.
I walked further inside. I saw a light flickering. Then some dolls crept behind me and I disappeared in a bloody room...

Lexie Hillebrant (9)
Yeo Moor Primary School, Clevedon

THE WEREWOLF

Once, on an eerie night when the moon was full, my rusty car broke down. As I stepped outside my car, lightning illuminated the forest below. Hurriedly, I walked along the curb, looking for help. Just then, I felt like I was being watched. I turned around. Nothing was there, but I still felt eyes were peering at me from the darkness. I turned around again. Two blazing red eyes glared back at me from the night. They soon rose out of sight. Suddenly, I felt some jagged teeth sharply pierce my neck. "A werewolf!" I cried...

Jack Wakefield-Paul (8)
Yeo Moor Primary School, Clevedon

DOLLS

One late night, a girl was walking and she saw a haunted house in a bloody graveyard with bent gates around it. The girl entered the haunted house and crept into the basement. She heard some whispering voices. Suddenly, the door slammed shut behind her. She turned around and there were bloody chains hanging from the roof. She looked at a shelf with dolls on. One of them moved! She ran to the door and tried to open it, but it wouldn't budge. The dolls chased after her. Suddenly, she tripped and fell onto a creaky floorboard...

Tia Andrea Neath (9)
Yeo Moor Primary School, Clevedon

SLENDER MAN

It was Friday the 13th at 3am. Me and my friends entered a graveyard and played spin the bottle. It landed on me. They dared me to summon Slender Man and it worked! His blank face was as white as snow.
As I ran further into the graveyard, I could hear my heart beating inside my chest rapidly. Then a thick fog rolled in so I couldn't see anything. I could just make out one of the Slender Man's pitch-black tentacles reaching out for other people. Speedily, I ran back to see who they were. My parents... They were dead!

Louisa Hoare (8)
Yeo Moor Primary School, Clevedon

THE GIRL AND THE VAMPIRE

Once upon a spooky Halloween night, there was a little girl called Lily. That night, Lily went to a 100-year-old abandoned school. When she opened the door and saw a zombie, she ran into the school and ran screaming down the corridor. Zombies chased after her. Lily ran into a classroom to hide.
When she went into the classroom, she discovered that it was a vampire's bedroom! Lily panicked and then the vampire grabbed her and started to suck her blood. Lily started to turn into a vampire and Lily was never seen again...

Megan Legge (7)
Yeo Moor Primary School, Clevedon

THE MIDNIGHT FIGURE

I was on a train heading for France at midnight and I was asleep. It was getting cold. Suddenly, the train jerked. I woke up. A hooded figure stood outside my carriage. Mysteriously, the door moved, creaking open without human touch. Before I could say anything, the figure opened a vast, swirly portal. All my things, along with the seats and windows, got sucked through! I had to dodge out the way of the portal. I finally managed to jump onto the figure and realised it was a hologram. I felt myself falling down, down, down...

Florence Ella Bosley-Brooks (8)
Yeo Moor Primary School, Clevedon

VENTRILOQUIST DUMMY

One Halloween, there was a boy called Zack. He went into a park. It wasn't just a park, it was a scary park! He crept inside and accidentally stepped on a twig. The dummy he was looking at suddenly turned around. The dummy told his monster friends to find the human. There were so many monsters: a yeti, a witch as big as a bus and a bloodthirsty werewolf with ripped pants. There was also a clown with a tiny hat and spotted clothes. So many monsters! Zack thought the werewolf was going to find him, but it didn't!

Erin Kay (8)
Yeo Moor Primary School, Clevedon

THE SCARY ZOMBIE AND SOPHIE

There once was a scary zombie and it was the middle of the night. Then there was a little girl called Sophie. It was Halloween. Sophie skipped to a house.
When Sophie got her candy, she turned around and suddenly, there was nobody there. There was one more house left. Sophie went to the house, but she didn't want to go inside. She heard a sound. Sophie heard somebody coming towards the door. Sophie didn't know who it was. She turned around and hid in a bush. She saw a boot and then she disappeared...

Julia Olivia Kos (8)
Yeo Moor Primary School, Clevedon

TRAIN SIMULATOR 2019

One evening, I was playing Train Simulator 2019 when I was suddenly transported to an abandoned, creepy island in a train! There was thick, black fog rolling in. Then, all of a sudden, orange, smoky clouds fell from the sky. I got out of the train. A platform appeared from nowhere in the steamy fog. Then a skeleton-faced train puffed into the station. I uncoupled the tender from the engine. Then I began to run. A zombie started the train. Another zombie knocked me out. I woke up. It was just Train Simulator 2019!

Matthew Scott (7)
Yeo Moor Primary School, Clevedon

THE SNARLING DOGS

In the middle of the night, Mog woke up to a cold breeze coming from the backyard. He felt afraid! He slowly walked to the backyard and saw lots of giant dogs sniffing for food. The dogs snarled and Mog jumped. He ran back into the house and hid under the bed. The dogs moved quickly, they snarled louder and began to search for Mog. Mog closed his eyes and stopped breathing in the hope that the dogs wouldn't find him. Mog felt a heavy panting on his face. He slowly opened his eyes and saw his mum kissing him!

Evie Nixon (8)
Yeo Moor Primary School, Clevedon

TRICK OR TREAT SURPRISE!

Last year, I went trick or treating with my friends. We decided to split up and see who could get the most sweets. I decided to go to my nanny's house. She always gave me lots of sweets. I set off.

As I wandered deeper into the forest, it started to get dark. To my surprise, my path was gone! I kept walking. Somehow, I stumbled across a barn. It was ivy-clad. Suddenly, *boom!* Heavy fog rolled in... The next thing I remember was waking up in a room. I spun around. *Where's the door?*

Lola Atkin (8)
Yeo Moor Primary School, Clevedon

ZOMBIES AND SHACKS

On a dark and gloomy night, an old shack sat surrounded by a deafening wood with sounds I had never heard before, sounds I hoped to never hear again. I slowly edged forwards towards the giant door and it just opened, so I went in.

Blood was on the floor, making me grimace in horror. Suddenly, a potion roared at me like a rocket. It smashed and some got in my mouth. After that, I wanted to try some brains! I did, but I kind of liked them. "I'm a zombie!" I said. I stayed in the shack...

Teddy Parkin (8)
Yeo Moor Primary School, Clevedon

THE VAMPIRE

It was almost Halloween and a little girl was getting some spooky and scary decorations from the frightening attic. She forgot one, so she went back up to the spooky attic.
Suddenly, the door locked and the little girl was really scared!
All of a sudden, she heard a screech on the dark floorboards. Then she saw a frightening vampire! The vampire had bloody teeth, a ripped top and a lost eye. She hid behind a big box and the vampire couldn't see her. Then the vampire saw her and walked over to her...

Alannah Lock (8)
Yeo Moor Primary School, Clevedon

Dolls And Spiders

When I was walking in the gleaming sun, the sky suddenly changed. I heard a noise coming, then I ran after that! I was running from a freaky doll. "Help!" I screamed. I hid in a house, in a room. I lost the doll. *Phew!* I found an old computer and I played on it until I saw a shadow. "Who are you?" I said.
It didn't look like the doll. When I turned around, I saw a humongous spider. It was poisonous and another doll came. When I looked closer, it was just my baby sister!

Shay Murray (7)
Yeo Moor Primary School, Clevedon

MONSTROUS CHURCH!

As I walked past the tall, broken church, purple clouds fell from the sky. Then I went over. The clouds disappeared. I went into the church and it freaked me out. There was a monster's funeral inside! I counted the monsters and stopped. There were 10,000 monsters there! The monsters looked at the door and then they saw me. I ran for my life but a werewolf caught up to me. Then suddenly, a blizzard started pouring from the sky. It was freezing cold. The snow started falling all over me. It was so deep...

Luke Care (8)
Yeo Moor Primary School, Clevedon

THE HAUNTED HOUSE

One lovely and peaceful day, I took a stroll around the countryside. Suddenly, I came across a freaky haunted house. There were shattered pieces of glass all over the ground. There was fog everywhere. It was starting to get hard to see.
When I stepped into the house, the door slammed shut! It was pitch-black, my heart was pounding. In the shadows, I saw a ginormous, black figure. It was chasing me! I ran upstairs and finally found a hiding place. I heard strange noises. They echoed around the room...

Jazmin Lion (8)
Yeo Moor Primary School, Clevedon

DOWN THE STREET!

Once upon a time, down an unusual street, was an old haunted house. Every now and then, cackling came out of the house, but nobody cared because not a soul had ever been in there.
One night, I was walking past the house and smelled a delicious smell. I could help but go inside. Once I was inside, I couldn't smell the smell anymore. I heard a click behind me and I couldn't see anything. I wanted to get out, but the door was locked. I was trapped! "Help!" Nobody came for me...

Lennard Bull (8)
Yeo Moor Primary School, Clevedon

THE MONSTER, BENDY

In the night, I brought my torch with me and slowly crept into the house. There was ripped fabric. I went into the living room. Suddenly, there was a thud. Creeping through the ceiling was ink. I thought it was going to be the end of me! I quickly ran upstairs, went into the closet and hid. The noise started to get closer and closer. *Who is it?* "Who are you?" I looked out. Oh, it was just my brother scaring me! I went downstairs and something was right behind me. "Uh-oh..."

Annabel Fear (9)
Yeo Moor Primary School, Clevedon

EMILY AND THE MAGIC MIRROR

One sunny morning, Emily was getting ready for school in the attic because that was where her bedroom was. Then she saw a bright light in her mirror, so she stepped inside. It was only a forest so she decided to take a walk when, all of a sudden, there was a howl from a pack of wolves running towards her. They jumped on her. Then she zoomed back to her bedroom, but the strange thing was, the time hadn't changed from when she went into the mirror! It was the same time and the same day of the month!

Evie Hopkinson (8)
Yeo Moor Primary School, Clevedon

FOREST MONSTERS AND THE ABANDONED HOUSE!

Once in a forest, I was walking and I saw a house. It didn't look like a normal house. In an instant, it became dark. I heard a sound. Then suddenly, some monster music started. I ran for it... too late. I heard footsteps. Suddenly, I saw a terrifying monster in front of me! For a moment, I thought it was my dad dressed up, but when I got closer, I realised it wasn't. It couldn't be real! I then tried to scream, but nothing came out. I turned and ran, then a massive spider was in a web...

Kilian Markus Bull (8)
Yeo Moor Primary School, Clevedon

SPOOKY STORY

On a dark, mysterious night, a boy started to walk slowly through the zombie forest. There were zombies everywhere around him. He jumped over all of them. The zombies were very fast, so they charged quickly. He tripped over a plank of wood as he was chased by the zombies. He kept on tripping over planks of wood. He then rolled them down the hill to crush the zombies. Then there were a load more zombies! He found some more planks of wood and rolled them down to catch them. The zombies all got crushed!

Tyler Haggett (8)
Yeo Moor Primary School, Clevedon

THE NOWHERE HOUSE

As I cautiously turned around, I saw a flash of green. I felt horrified. The floor squeaked.
"Hello?"
Suddenly, I fell down. I landed on a broken bed. Just then, I saw lots of bugs. I ran, but running was a big mistake. A giant spider appeared, then I noticed that I fell every ten minutes. I fell once again and found myself in a room of doors. "Find the right exit," said a voice.
I fell again and woke up in my bed. I was confused. Was I free? What would happen next?

Chloe Rugman (9)
Yeo Moor Primary School, Clevedon

THE WEREWOLF AND THE BOY

Once upon a time, there was a boy. He sat down on a bench and heard something. He went to a spooky house and the door vanished in a flash. Where was the door? Out of nowhere, a dark figure with lots of hair appeared. He started running after the boy. He froze. *Snap!* The boy fell. He fell and hit the figure's foot. He then felt something furry on his leg. The boy then was pulled up the stairs, into the bedroom and then dragged up into the attic by the figure. It was a werewolf...

Jacob Puttick (8)
Yeo Moor Primary School, Clevedon

THE CLOWN

I walked through the field, but then I saw an abandoned house. A clown was looking out the window at me! Goosebumps grew on my arm. I turned around and a horde of zombies was walking towards me! I ran.
I reached the abandoned house. The clown was gone, but the horde was still coming! The horde surrounded me. The only way out was to go inside the house. I freaked out, but I still went in. The clown stood inside. I fainted and woke up on a chair, tied to it. The clown opened the door...

Franek Szpakowski (9)
Yeo Moor Primary School, Clevedon

THE DRAGON IN THE BASEMENT

A boy went into a haunted house. He went into the basement at 3am! The floor was cracking and he saw a monstrous dragon. It had two heads! Suddenly, the dragon started to wake up. Then a werewolf attacked the dragon. The boy ran away, straight into the Grim Reaper. He had a black hood and a face like a skull. The Grim Reaper slapped him with his sharp stick. The boy tried to talk to him, but the Grim Reaper didn't listen. The boy never came out of the house and was never seen again...

Franky Wright (8)
Yeo Moor Primary School, Clevedon

SCARY WEREWOLF

Once there was a girl walking through the woods and a ghost came out of the bushes. It scared her. She fell onto the floor and the ghost took her into a haunted house!
She woke up screaming and crept through the house. In one room, she saw dead people, but then she heard a noise. It was a wolf on a hill. She saw sharp teeth and the werewolf was looking at her. When it ran towards her, she felt petrified. He was actually just a cute doggy. He licked her face and she giggled loudly.

Olivia Palka (7)
Yeo Moor Primary School, Clevedon

THE WITCH'S CAULDRON

Once upon a time, there was an old haunted house with dirty bits and bobs. On the house were leaves and vines. When I went in, there was a mouldy apple on the side, but I took no notice of it and carried on searching. In the kitchen was burnt toast with jam on top. I heard the doorknob move, so I ran upstairs and hid under a big bed. Suddenly, I saw two huge feet, so I covered my eyes and, when I looked again, they were gone. Something squeezed my leg and it said, "Hello..."

Cassidy Backhouse (9)
Yeo Moor Primary School, Clevedon

THE THREE VAMPIRES

There once was a boy in a horrid graveyard named Harry. He got bitten by a vampire and Harry became a boy vampire. Then one of Harry's friends came over, his name was Dillon. One of Dillon's friends came too, his name was Isaac. Isaac ran to find Dillon, but he was nowhere to be found. Harry bit Dillon, then Dillon became a vampire. Then Harry and Dillon hid. They jumped out at Isaac and bit him.
At night, they had a party and everybody celebrated and everybody cheered!

Harry Pow (7)
Yeo Moor Primary School, Clevedon

THE ABANDONED SCHOOL

On Friday the 13th, Teddy went to an abandoned school and there was a key on the floor. There were a lot of cobwebs and one was huge! There was a graveyard with blood and zombie hands sticking out of the ground. Teddy opened the door using the key.
Then he saw Boldy and Teddy ran. Teddy ran as fast as he could and hid in a classroom. He hid there for an hour. Then Boldy found Teddy again! Teddy started to run and lost Boldy and now he was surrounded by zombies and spiders...

Callum Wright (8)
Yeo Moor Primary School, Clevedon

ME AND THE WITCH

Once I was running in the forest when it went dark. I couldn't see anything, it was the middle of the night. Then I saw a slimy house in the middle of nothing. Then a green, old hand opened the window. I tried to hide as quickly as I could, but it was too late!
The next day, I woke up in a really old castle. It wasn't fun. I tried and tried to get out. Suddenly, a witch's cackle came out of the kitchen. It was a witch making a potion with some of my hair...

Matylda Szpakowska (7)
Yeo Moor Primary School, Clevedon

THE LAST MOMENTS OF MY LIFE

Quietly, I crept down a cracked path that led to a vast house. Without knowing who owned the house, I went to go in. I reached the door, curious about what was in store for me. As I got about ten paces inside the house, the door closed with a creak. As soon as I heard this, I felt a shiver down my spine. I looked around, checking I wasn't being followed. As I walked further into the unknown, I saw some stairs and, at the same time, the door opened. I heard footsteps...

Alex Kizilis (8)
Yeo Moor Primary School, Clevedon

THE MYSTERIOUS RAILWAY

On a dark night, I came to a railway. No one was there. Trains were moving on their own, no drivers or passengers. I looked behind me only to see a hideous ghost! I ran as fast as I could. The ghost chased me everywhere I went. But when I touched a train, my hand went through the train, but the ghost didn't. When the ghost followed me, he instantly vanished. In front of me was another ghost, so I ran out of the railway only to see the railway vanish forever...

Kian Murray (8)
Yeo Moor Primary School, Clevedon

THE ABANDONED HOUSE!

One bright morning, I was asleep in my bed. All of a sudden, I blinked and found myself in an empty house. I got out of bed. My body shivered. I crept downstairs and heard a witch's laugh. I nervously said, "Hello? Is anyone there?"
I saw up ahead, things falling from shelves. Then my family were knocked out! I went into an empty room. The door creaked. When I opened it, a dark figure was looking out the window. It turned and looked at me...

Edward Kerslake (8)
Yeo Moor Primary School, Clevedon

THE DEMON CHURCH

One beautiful day, I walked past an old church, so I thought I could go in there that night. The sun went down, the moon came up. It was time for me to go into the church! As I walked in, a cracking noise came from the main room. I ran to the basement and saw a figure. It was dark with red, glowing eyes. I ran into a very, very small room. I saw the figure running for me, so I ran out of the church. I ran for home and said, "Home! Home! Home!"

Noah Leylan Mitchell (8)
Yeo Moor Primary School, Clevedon

THE SPOOKY STORY

One day, I was walking to the church in the darkness. It was scary. I heard noises around me but there was nobody in the church. I walked around. Suddenly, I saw something, so I said hello. It walked close to me, so I backed up and it was singing creepily. I ran to the bathroom and locked the door. It was banging on the door. It was a doll, a creepy doll with cracks on its face!
I sneaked slowly to the kitchen and got a pan to scare it off...

Hannah Harries (8)
Yeo Moor Primary School, Clevedon

DEADLY DANGER!

One night, I had to go to the shop. I got there and I went out of the shop. But suddenly, it was dark and, on the way home, I saw an abandoned house. I went closer and closer. A light turned on by itself. Then I went closer and all the lights turned on by themselves. I then heard monster and zombie music playing. I ran and ran, but I couldn't get away because there was a deep, dark forest nearby. I had to go in, I had to do the right thing...

Cai Douglas Anderson (8)

Yeo Moor Primary School, Clevedon

SHELTER

On a dark, gloomy night, I was walking through the woods. It started raining. I saw a cave in the distance. I went to shelter in the cave. The wind blew the rain into the cave, so I moved deeper and deeper into the cave. Suddenly, I saw red eyes glaring at me. I heard a loud, scary growl. I jumped, my heart was pumping. It was a ginormous, vicious cave bear! I ran as fast as Usain Bolt out of the cave into the sloppy mud. I went face first!

William Came (7)
Yeo Moor Primary School, Clevedon

DAD

One night, a girl and her dad were watching a film. Her dad got popcorn to eat. The dad told the girl it was time for bed. When the girl was sleeping, the dad changed into a monster! He had four eyes and ten legs. The dad said, "Wahahaha!"
He went into the girl's room. Can you guess what happened? The girl saw it was her dad and he then turned back into her dad!

Constanca Flores (7)
Yeo Moor Primary School, Clevedon

THE CREEPY DOLL

One bright and sunny day, I went to the forest with my mum. Then, out of the corner of my eye, I saw a doll. I went back to see if she was there and she freaked me out because she had cracks all over her. I decided to leave her there. She kept following us everywhere, so we decided to go home.
Uh oh! She followed us home so Mum drove her somewhere far away...

Milana Grabinska (9)
Yeo Moor Primary School, Clevedon

THE ROOM OF DARKNESS

On a very dark night, I was walking down a quiet street. It was very quiet and then suddenly I heard a crack... then it stopped so I sat down. All of a sudden, I got pulled into a pitch-black room. The clock struck midnight and killer clowns, zombies and dolls were everywhere! I then realised I was locked in forever...

Bobby Sansum Snook (8)
Yeo Moor Primary School, Clevedon

YOUNG WRITERS INFORMATION

We hope you have enjoyed reading this book – and that you will continue to in the coming years.

If you're a young writer who enjoys reading and creative writing, or the parent of an enthusiastic poet or story writer, do visit our website **www.youngwriters.co.uk**. Here you will find free competitions, workshops and games, as well as recommended reads, a poetry glossary and our blog. There's lots to keep budding writers motivated to write!

If you would like to order further copies of this book, or any of our other titles, then please give us a call or order via your online account.

Young Writers
Remus House
Coltsfoot Drive
Peterborough
PE2 9BF
(01733) 890066
info@youngwriters.co.uk

Join in the conversation!
Tips, news, giveaways and much more!

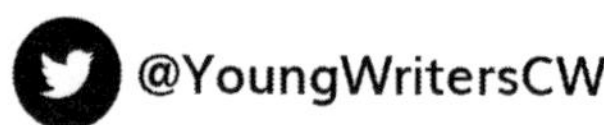